INSTRUCTIONS

For Louis

LITTLE TIGER PRESS
An imprint of Magi Publications
1 The Coda Centre, 189 Munster Road, London SW6 6AW
www.littletigerpress.com
First published in Great Britain 2002
2002 © Diane and Christyan Fox
Diane and Christyan Fox have asserted their rights to
be identified as the author and illustrator of this work
under the Copyright, Designs and Patents Act, 1988.
Printed in Singapore · All rights reserved
ISBN 1 85430 769 X
3 5 7 9 10 8 6 4 2

Spaceman PiggyWiggy

Christyan and Diane Fox

LITTLE TIGER PRESS

Whenever I lie in bed at night, I look at the stars above, and dream of what it would be like to be a daring spaceman!

I would climb into my rocket dressed in my special spacesuit  and prepare for lift-off.

I would need
lots of training
to learn how
to use all
the controls.
Then...

Blast off into
outer space!

In space
everything floats . . .

so it would be very difficult to eat and drink!

I would have to go outside the spaceship . . .

for a space walk.

We would land on exciting, faraway planets...

and make new friends.

But I hope there would be time to do all these things . . .